Text copyright © Sally Grindley 1998
Illustrations copyright © Tania Hurt-Newton 1998

First published in Great Britain in 1998
by Macdonald Young Books
an imprint of Wayland Publishers Ltd
61 Western Road
Hove
East Sussex
BN3 1JD

Find Macdonald Young Books on the internet at http://www.myb.co.uk

The right of Sally Grindley to be identified as the author of this Work
and the right of Tania Hurt-Newton to be identified as the illustrator of this Work
has been asserted by them in accordance with the Copyright, Designs and
Patents Act 1988.

Printed in Hong Kong by Wing King Tong.

British Library Cataloguing in Publication Data available

ISBN 0 7500 2508 5

SALLY GRINDLEY

MULBERRY
home alone

Illustrated by Tania Hurt-Newton

MACDONALD YOUNG BOOKS

The front door slammed shut. Mulberry
stood in the hall and looked puzzled.
Where was his pat on the head?
He scratched at the door and whined.
He barked and then he howled.
Nobody came.

He ran to the window.
They were climbing inside the car.
"Did you mean to leave me?" he
barked. "Did you forget to pat me on
the head? Did you forget to say 'Be
good, Mulberry'?" Nobody heard.

The car drove away.
Mulberry lay down on the floor
with his chin on his paws and sulked.
He didn't like being home alone.

Mulberry could see his squeaky ball
under the table.

"I'm coming to get you," he growled.

He pounced on it and threw it across
the room. He galloped after it and
knocked into a chair.

The chair fell over on to a plant.
The plant crashed to the floor.

He bit off a few leaves.
"I'm hungry," he whimpered.

Mulberry trotted into the kitchen.
His bowl was empty.
"Who's eaten my doggy crunchy
things?" he growled.

Then he remembered where they kept
the packet. He went to the cupboard
and closed his teeth round the handle.

Then he pulled,
GRRRRRR!
and pulled,
GRRRRRR!
and pulled
GRRRRRR!
until the cupboard door flew open.

Mulberry fell backwards and knocked
over the rubbish bin. Rubbish spilled
all over the floor. Some of it smelt
good. Some of it smelt like food.
Mulberry stuck his nose in and pulled
out a piece of meat – YUM! and some
cheese – YUM!

He dragged the packet from the
cupboard. The packet burst and
doggy crunchy things flew over the
floor. Mulberry crunched his way
round the kitchen until there was
nothing left. Then he sat down in
his basket.

"Time for a nap," he yawned, and he fell asleep.

Mulberry was woken by a tap-tapping sound. He knew that sound – CAT! He leapt from his basket and ran into the kitchen, barking loudly.

Cat's head was poking through the cat flap. "Oh no you don't!" barked Mulberry. Cat's head disappeared. Mulberry sat and

waited. Cat's paw rattled the cat flap.

Scaredy cat, scaredy cat!

"You're not coming in," growled Mulberry. "I'm in charge here." Nothing happened. "What's the matter? Are you scared?" he barked. Still nothing happened.

Mulberry wandered back into the other room. He began to chew up a newspaper. The cat flap banged. He rushed into the kitchen and there was Cat, in the kitchen!

Cat stared at Mulberry. Mulberry stared at Cat. He crouched down low, he waggled his bottom, then he pounced.

Cat leapt in the air. She spat at
Mulberry and shot off upstairs.
Mulberry skidded on an empty can and
landed in a mess of spaghetti hoops.
He leapt after Cat.

But he couldn't find her.
He looked behind the curtains.
Cat wasn't there.
He looked under a pile of clothes.
Cat wasn't there.
He jumped up into a funny little bed
that he hadn't seen before.
Cat wasn't there.

Then he looked under the big bed.
Cat was there, right in the middle,
but Mulberry couldn't reach her. She
stared at him and washed her paws.
Mulberry pretended he didn't care.

He grabbed a slipper in his mouth
and pretended it was Cat. He shook it
and shook it and growled. Then he
carried it to the top of the stairs and
dropped it down.

It landed on a vase of flowers which fell to the ground and broke. Water spilled over the rug in the hall.

Mulberry ran downstairs, slipped on the rug and knocked over the telephone table.

Just then he heard a banging noise.
He knew that noise.
They were back!
Mulberry ran to the window.
He heard the key turn in the door.

He ran into the hall and skidded on the rug. The door opened and he leapt at them.

"Hello, hello!" he barked.
"I've been home alone!
You forgot to pat me on the head!
You forgot my doggy crunchy things!
You forgot to say 'Be good, Mulberry'!"

"Good boy, Mulberry," they said.
And then, "Bad dog, Mulberry.
Go to your basket and stay there."
Mulberry looked at them and blinked.

"Bad dog. Look at this mess," they said.
Mulberry hung his tail between his legs.
He went to his basket, put his chin on
his paws, and sulked.

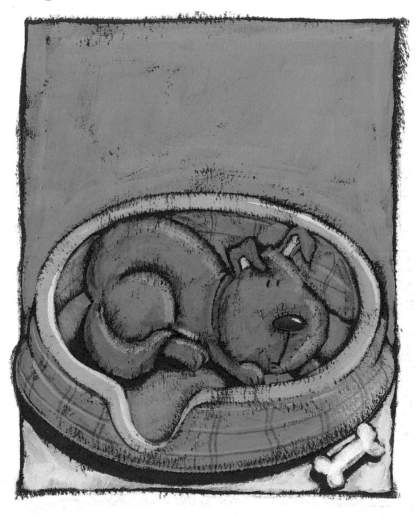

Then he saw something new. There was another basket on the floor and it was shaking. Was Cat inside? Mulberry crept towards it and growled. The basket moved again.

Mulberry howled and hid under the stairs. They came running.

They picked up the thing in the basket and patted it and spoke kind words. Mulberry shook in his hiding place. He was frightened. Where were *his* kind words?

At last the WAAAH! WAAAH!
WAAAH! stopped.
Mulberry peeped out and whimpered.
They came to find him. They patted
him on the head.

"It's all right, Mulberry," they said.
"There's nothing to be frightened of.
Come and have some doggy bones."
Mulberry bounded from his hiding
place and leapt up at them.

"Good boy, Mulberry," they said.
"We forgive you."
Mulberry crunched his doggy bones.
Then they took him for his walk
like they always did. They threw him
a stick like they always did. He settled
down to sleep like he always did.
And he felt safe again.

But it was a long time before he would go anywhere near the thing in the basket that went WAAAH!

Look out for more fun titles in the First Storybook series.

Mulberry Alone in the Park *by Sally Grindley*

The front door has been left open. It must be doggy walkies time for Mulberry. So off he trots to the park. He has great fun chasing squirrels and doggy-paddling after the ducks. But then it starts to get dark. Mulberry is woken by a loud bang, then another. Bright colours light up the sky. Maybe being alone in the park is not such fun after all...

Leon's Fancy Dress Day *by Alan MacDonald*

Leon doesn't know what to wear to the fancy dress parade. All his friends have picked the best ideas. Then he finds a black mask in his toy box. He decides to go as a big bad robber. But nobody is very scared and Leon can't see where he's going. How is he ever going to win a prize?

Leon Gets A Scarecut *by Alan MacDonald*

Leon must get his mane cut for Patsy's party. On the way to Sid's Barber Shop he meets some friends. Strangely they are all wearing new hats. Leon is a little nervous as Sid's new electric trimmer buzzes in his ears. He closes his eyes until it's over. Then he looks in the mirror. Help! He can't go to Patsy's party with a scarecut-haircut!

All these books and many more in the Storybook series can be purchased from your local bookseller. For more information about Storybooks, write to: *The Sales Department, Macdonald Young Books, 61 Western Road, Hove, East Sussex BN3 1JD.*